SINCERELY, Harriet

SARAH WINIFRED SEARLE

Graphic Universe™ • Minneapolis

For the cool librarians of Kennebunk Free Library, who introduced this reluctant reader to a broader world of graphic novels, zines, and other books that felt like they were made just for her

Graphic Universe™
A division of Lerner Publishing Group, Inc.
241 First Avenue North
Minneapolis, MN 55401 USA

For reading levels and more information, look up this title at www.lernerbooks.com.

Library of Congress Cataloging-in-Publication Data

Names: Searle, Sarah Winifred, author, illustrator.
Title: Sincerely, Harriet / Sarah Winifred Searle.
Description: Minneapolis : Graphic Universe, [2019] | Summary: In 1996 Chicago, thirteen-year-old Harriet Flores, living with boredom, loneliness, and a chronic illness, lets her imagination run wild—with mixed results—and learns about the power of storytelling.
Identifiers: LCCN 2018014447 (print) | LCCN 2018021004 (ebook) | ISBN 9781541542723 (eb pdf) | ISBN 9781512440195 (lb : alk. paper) | ISBN 9781541545298 (pb : alk. paper)
Subjects: LCSH: Graphic novels. | CYAC: Graphic novels. | Hispanic Americans—Fiction. | Imagination—Fiction. | Multiple sclerosis—Fiction.
Classification: LCC PZ7.7.S417 (ebook) | LCC PZ7.7.S417 Si 2019 (print) | DDC 741.5/973—dc23

LC record available at https://lccn.loc.gov/2018014447

Manufactured in the United States of America
1-42281-26138-9/14/2018

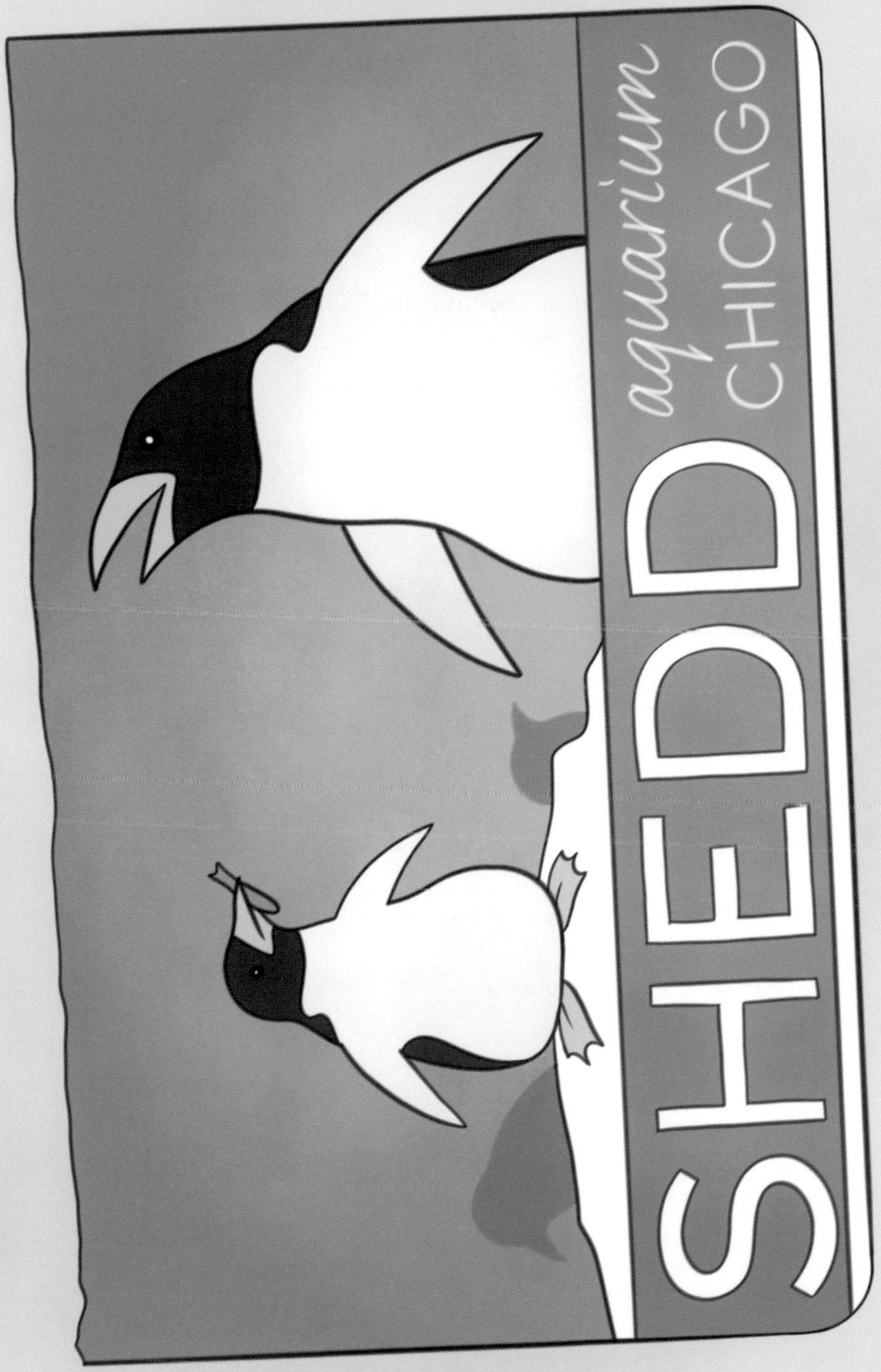
SHEDD
aquarium
CHICAGO

Hannah!
Sorry I couldn't come to camp this year, really wish I could but we had to move to Chicago. It's ok so far, kinda weird not having a car. Today we went to the aquarium! The penguins are super cute. How are you? How's camp? Is Ashley there? Say hi for me. You have to eat 100 burnt marshmallows in my honor. Each. No cheating!
♡ Harriet

Hannah Baum
Pine Point Camp
1 Pine Point Rd
Greencrest, IN 46511

Mom! How are you? How was your day?

Good, good. Yours? How's that summer reading going?

Boooring.

Well, Harriet, once you get it over with, we'll treat you to something more fun. Deal?

...Deal.

You know I hate leaving you, babe. We'll have a family day out soon. *Promise.*

Ah, shoot. Running late again.

Go ahead and make something from the freezer if Dad's not home by eight. Love you!

sssshhhhhhssssshhhhhhh
No such thing as ghosts!
sshhshhhhh

Pancakes!

With blue-berries?

Blueberries!

Since when are you such a morning person?

I dunno.

Pancakes? Rad.

Oh, so, Luca from the garage said his friends are looking for a drummer. He's getting their demo for me to check out.

Heck yeah!

Not sure how practice times would line up with my bartending schedule, though...

Have a good day!

Love you.

20

I keep some treats around for the grandkids. Have as much as you like.

Thanks.

I'll select photos, then you'll paste them in and make sure they're nice and straight. Sound good?

Got it.

I'm putting this album together for my grandson.

So he always knows where his family comes from, and someday he can share it with his children.

But...do you want to know a secret?

Hmm?

I do it so I can try to remember better too.

ha ha

I can't recall their names for the life of me, and I thought my wedding was supposed to be the best day of my life.

Good thing it wasn't. If I'd hit the high point of my life at nineteen, I wouldn't have had much happiness left over for the next sixty years and counting.

Bleh.

Double bleh. Why did I ever try to like this stuff?

Brett dishes on his new rom-com role

TeenTown: So Brett, tell us about your new flick!

...amaville is about a... ...f misfit studen...

TeenTown: Mind sharing any juicy details of your award-nominated kiss with Winona?

Brett: (Laughs.) Cut to the chase, why don't ya!

Brett: She's so professional, I don't want to divulge too much. But I will say that she uses this fruity lip balm – cherry, maybe? – and I'll always remember her for it.

Fine, I guess. But I have my suspicions.

No one lives on the third floor, right? Haven't you wondered what's up there?

Storage?

I hear weird noises when I'm alone, and at night, and...what if...

What if something weird happened here? What if it's *haunted*?

34

We've talked about this.

How do you think Pearl would feel if she knew you said something like that about her?

Has she ever been anything but kind to you?

I'm sorry.

Don't be sorry. Bc *better.*

Now...I think we've got a little ice cream left, if you still have room.

Ice cream!

Thank heavens that heat wave broke. Gorgeous day.

Is this one of Abuelita's tapes? What did she send this time?

Half an episode of that old puppet show and a couple music videos so far.

Nice.

I'm sorry, you must be so bored. I thought I'd have more time after training, but apparently overtime isn't optional.

Figures.

Yeah. I understand.

I was thinking, what if we signed you up for a summer activity thing so you could start meeting other kids? Sports and crafts and stuff.

Really?

Really. After a nap. A nice, long...

snnnorrk

Hey, I'm trying to read, here!

whap

You finally get started on that reading?

Yep.

Good. How many pages?

Like, at least fifty! Maybe even a hundred.

Did we get any mail?

No, but...

41

Thanks.

Room for another? I've got a sec before I have to get ready.

How does he pick his nose with such pointy fingers?

Mooom!

squeeeaaaaak

Whoa.

Maybe the *ghost* wrote this.

Um...watch movies. Read some, too. I've got catching up to do before school starts.

What kind of reading?

So, how do you entertain yourself while your folks are at work?

Eh. I know it's supposed to be important or something, but...

Right now, *The Great Gatsby.*

Ah. Not a fan, I take it?

It doesn't feel like it was written for *me,* if that makes sense.

Um, I was wondering...what's on the third floor?

Storage.

No one's ever lived up there?

Well, yes, a long time ago. Not since my children moved out, though.

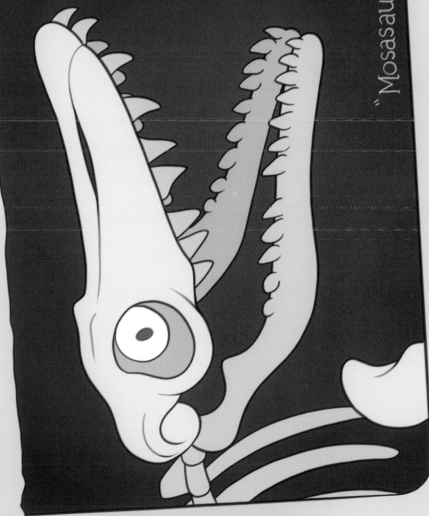

"Mosasaurus"

Dear Hannah,

How's camp so far? I miss flashlight tag and swimming and all that stuff, but we've been busy here, too. I made a friend, I bet you'd think he's _really_ cute. Why don't you and Ashley visit before school starts? We can all hang out together and Nick can show us some cool places around the city! ♡ Harriet

Hannah Baum

Pine Point Camp

1 Pine Point Rd

Greencrest, IN 46511

Mary Lennox has her flaws, yes. But that's part of what makes her story so satisfying.

She grows a lot over the course of the book.

Mm.

You didn't read it, did you?

Expecting something?

No.

Just thinking about that weird mailman.

What's weird about him?

Just a feeling. He's always creeping around people's houses...

Yes, so he can deliver their mail.

Have you seen the way he glares at the dogs across the street? It's like he's plotting something...*evil.*

Harriet...

I've known Gary Ganesh since he was born, and there isn't an ounce of cunning in that man.

He's nervous around dogs because the Jones's Chihuahua bit him when he was a kid. Almost lost his little finger.

Sorry if that's not much of a dark backstory, but if you enjoy the macabre, I could ask him to show you the scar.

N-no, that's okay.

Or, you know, you could write your *own* story about an evil mailman and make it as exciting as you want.

It gets easier with practice. Start with something you know.

Writing's *hard*.

Write about your life. See what happens.

Maybe.

My name is Harriet Alejandra Flores, I'm thirteen years old, and I hope we can be friends.

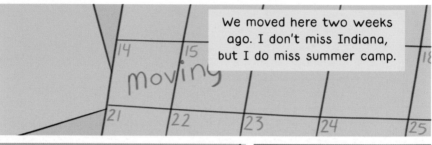

We moved here two weeks ago. I don't miss Indiana, but I do miss summer camp.

moving

14 15 18

21 22 23 24 25

I understand why we needed to move here, but school doesn't start for almost another month, and I can't be at camp with Ashley and Hannah, and Mom and Papa are so busy with their new jobs when I just want to have a good summer, you know?

See, I've been homeschooled for the past two years. I had friends before, but we lost touch when I got sick. Camp was the first (and last) time I got to really hang out with other kids and have fun in forever.

68

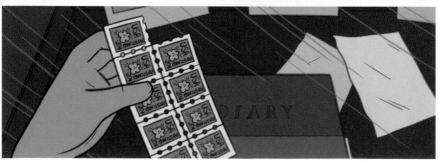

NOK
NOK

So, what are you up to today?

Trying to read *Of Mice and Men.*

Ah, a nice short one. What do you think so far?

Meh. I'm tired of books with boring girl characters who don't get to do anything.

Aren't we both. What else is on your reading list?

Lord of the Flies, old Greek thing, um... *Mockingbird?*

To Kill a Mockingbird?

Yeah.

74

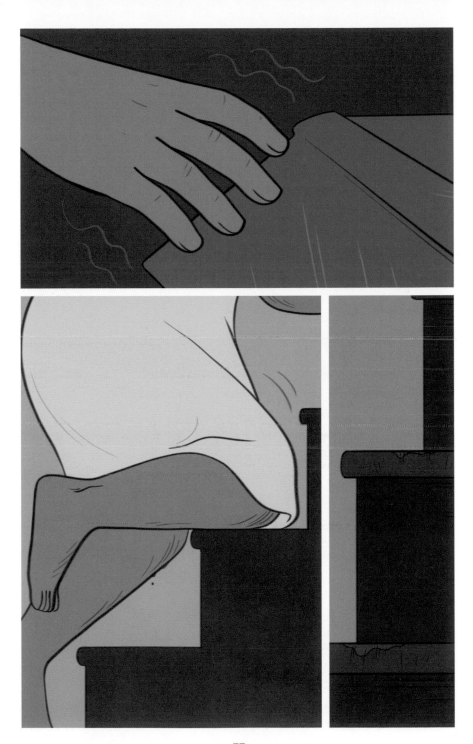

Fine!

I mean, the usual, I guess. Yours?

Oh, the usual.

You've been quiet lately.

Well, you're the one who kept telling me to get my reading done.

I don't remember picking up that one at the library.

Pearl lent it to me.

Really? Cool.

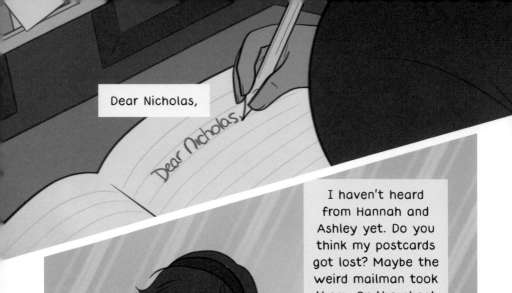

Dear Nicholas,

I haven't heard from Hannah and Ashley yet. Do you think my postcards got lost? Maybe the weird mailman took them. Or the ghost in this house is hiding them.

Or maybe they're just too busy to write, I guess.

Hannah's always busy because she's friends with everyone ever. Her parents sent her lots of snacks and magazines that she always shared with our whole cabin, just because she's nice like that.

Ashley is Hannah's best friend. She's cool, too. Really cool.

Dinner in five, Harry! Can you help set the table?

B-be right there, Papa!

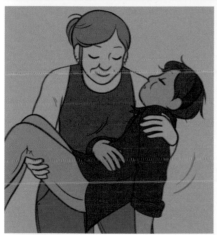

Sweet dreams.

You two seem pretty tuckered out. Did I miss some excitement?

Oh, nothing much, just a ragin' party. The whole neighborhood was here.

Darn.

sigh

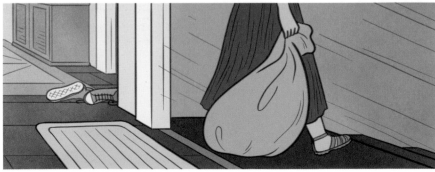

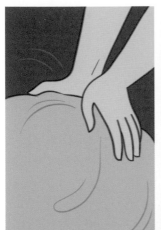

So *that's* where the dumbwaiter goes.

So, what do you think of *To Kill a Mockingbird* so far?

It's, um...

...I haven't really started it yet. Sorry.

Well, let me know when you get there.

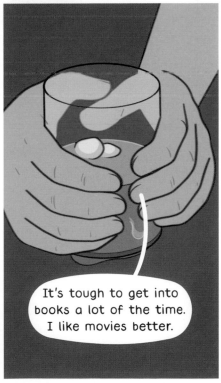

It's tough to get into books a lot of the time. I like movies better.

I suppose they're not all that different, are they? Just different ways to tell stories.

I'll always find it easier to lose myself in a good book more than anything else, but I can respect a good film.

Are there any that have stuck with you, Harriet?

I don't know.

Are there any stories that have lingered in your mind, even long after finishing them?

I don't...

How about this: Do you have a favorite?

Yeah. I mean, it changes, but... *Beetlejuice,* maybe?

I can see that. It's about a girl who moves into a weird old house, right? That must resonate with you about now.

I guess? I mean...I don't know.

Stories are good company, aren't they? Always there for us when we need them.

It must be hard, being away from your friends. But school starts again in a few weeks, you'll meet new kids—

Stop.

You don't know me. You don't know *anything.*

Harriet—

I gotta go finish my chores.

She just doesn't get it.

rustle CLINK

Junk,
junk...

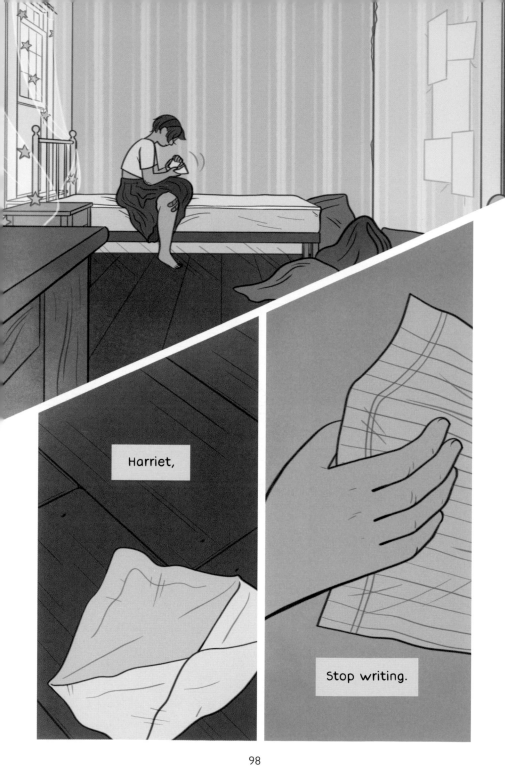

Your camp friends'll write back soon, I'm sure.

You'll see.

Yeah.

Dear Hannah,

I'm going to be pretty busy for a while, so this is probably my last postcard for now, and you might want to put off any visits you were planning. Maybe after school starts. Anyway, I hope the rest of camp is fun.

ts/Asht

Sincerely,
Harriet

Hannah Baum
Pine Point Camp
1 Pine Point Rd
Greencrest, IN 46511

104

Cherry.

With sprinkles!

This seems like as good a moment as any to share some news.

News?

My boss agreed to let me out of overtime if I use it to finally finish my nursing degree. I start classes in a few weeks.

That's so great!

Congrats, hon.

Love you two so much!

Gross!

I wish we made tortillas more often. They're so much better than the ones from the store.

Well, they're a heck of a lot of work. I like keeping them for special occasions.

But hey, while we're celebrating, how about champurrado for dessert?

Mmm.

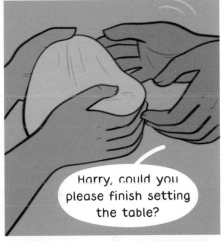

Harry, could you please finish setting the table?

CRSSH!

I need you to be honest.

Have you been clumsy lately?

No!

I'm fine.

Harry? What's wrong?

Nothing!

tch

I don't think I can ask for time off yet. Getting out of overtime was hard enough.

If you call the doctor in the morning, I can squeeze out early to take her in. Just ring the garage to let me know what time.

All right. Thanks.

Dear Nicholas,

I probably owe you an apology. I'm sorry I haven't been 100% truthful with you...

But I think I lie to myself more than anyone else.

I wanted Hannah and Ashley to be my friends so bad. I thought if I acted like they were, it could happen for real.

I was wrong.

I'm only telling you this because you're not real. Or, well, you're real, but you'll never see this.

I can't talk to my parents.

They think I'm scared of being sick, but it's not really that. They don't understand, just like Pearl.

I think *you'd* understand, though.

I know it wouldn't be how I imagine it, but...

I wish we could meet.

1:30. Got it.

Thanks.

Pearl mentioned she could use your help today...

How about you go down there after you finish your breakfast?

Mom will be back around lunchtime to pick you up.

'Kay.

Love you! Can't wait to get home tonight!

Love you too.

Okay, here we go!

Oh, come on! There have got to be stairs to the third floor *somewhere*.

How else would Nicholas have gotten up to his room?

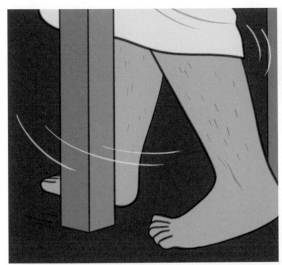

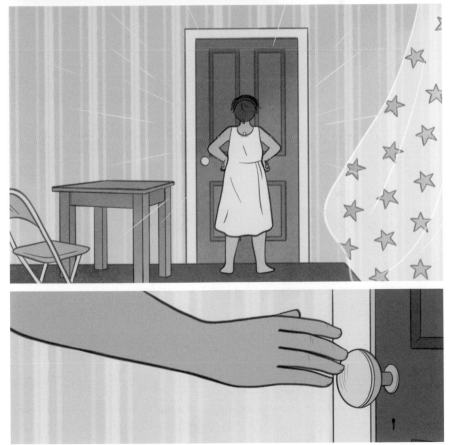

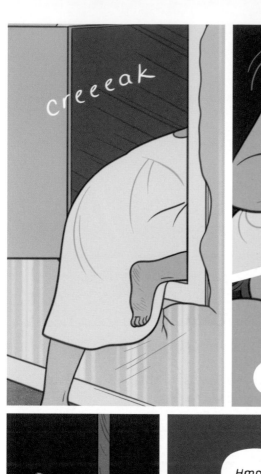

creeeak

Whew.

Hmph!

Nicholas?

ssshhhshhhh

N-nothing to be scared of!

This was silly, anyway. Of course he isn't up here. Unless...

creak

shh

ssh

No. There's no Nicholas. No ghosts, either.

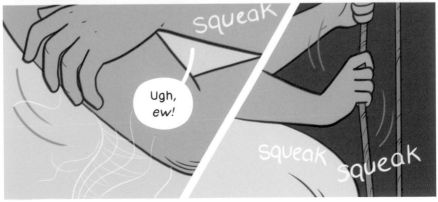

squeak

Ugh, *ew!*

squeak squeak

Are you *sure* you feel all right? I can't believe you weren't seriously injured.

What on God's Earth were you doing, playing in that thing?

I... I don't know.

Your father told me about what's going on, what you've all been through. I offered to help keep an eye on you.

I'm sorry I couldn't do that for you.

I know talking to me isn't the same as talking to someone your own age, but I like to think we're friends.

I *hope* we can be friends, anyway.

I'm sorry.

It's okay.

No, it's not! I've been a *jerk!*

I'm sorry I scared you today.

I'm sorry I was rude to you last time.

I'm sorry I said your house smells funny, and I'm sorry I told Mom you might be a murder lady.

All water under the bridge, my dear.

Now, how about some lemonade?

Lemonade!

I'd like to give you something special to read this time.

It was Nicky's favorite book when he was in quarantine...

...and I hope it'll keep *you* good company too.

PETER & WENDY

I'd like you to keep it. I'm sure he won't mind.

NOK NOK

That'll be your mother.

Thank
you.

'But who is he, my pe—'

'He is Peter Pan, you know, mother.'

At first Mrs. Darling did not know, but after thinking back into her childhood she just remembered a Peter Pan who was said to live with the fairies. There were odd stories about him; as that when children died he went part of the way with them, so that they should not be frightened. She had believed in him at the time, but now that she was married and full of sense she quite doubted whether there was any such person.

'Besides,' she said to Wendy, 'he would be grown up by this time.'

'Oh no, he isn't grown up,' Wendy assured her confidently, 'and he is just my size.' She meant that he was her size in both mind and body; she didn't know how she knew it, she just knew it.

Mrs. Darling consulted Mr. Darling, but he smiled pooh-pooh. 'Mark my words,' he said, 'it is some nonsense Nana has been putting into their heads; just the sort of idea a dog would have. I

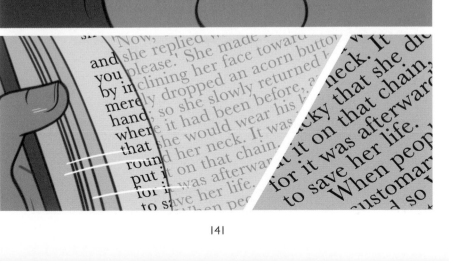

and she replied 'Now, you please.' She made face toward by inclining her face toward merely dropped an acorn button hand; so she slowly returned where it had been before, a neck. It that she would wear his that round her neck. It was lucky that she did put it on that chain. for it was afterward for it was afterward to save her life. to save her life. When people and so

The [...] ld be subl[...] [...]ed across the wat[...] [...]was to be heard a sound [...] musical and the most melanchol[...] world: the mermaids calling to the moo[...]

Peter was not quite like other boys; but he was afraid at last. A tremor ran through him, like a shudder passing over the sea; but on the sea one shudder follows another till there are hundreds of them, and Peter felt just the one. Next moment he was standing erect on the rock again, with that smile on his face and a drum beating within him. It was saying, 'To die will be an awfully big adventure!'

...Is this how you felt, Nicholas?

sssssshhhh

I don't want to feel like that.

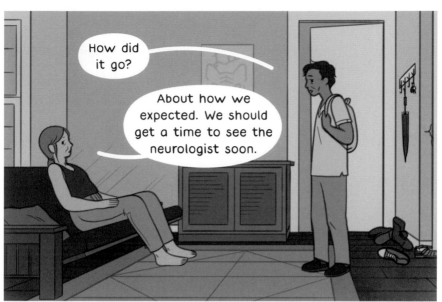

I tried writing in the diary, but it didn't work. I want to talk for real.

We're here for you, honey.

You don't talk about it much, but I know you miss music.

And I don't want Papa to have to quit school again because of my MS.

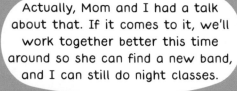

Actually, Mom and I had a talk about that. If it comes to it, we'll work together better this time around so she can find a new band, and I can still do night classes.

I don't regret taking time off with you even a little, Harriet. And don't worry. This time, it really feels right to go back.

Really?

We're both going back to school in a few weeks, *together*.

Let's go supply shopping! How about you pick me out one of those sparkly zipper binders, so the other kids know I'm cool?

Heh, yeah.

Is there anything else on your mind?

What if I don't make any friends?

It might take some time to find the right people, but—

No, Mom. You don't get it.

Thank you for talking to us.

It's okay to be sad and scared sometimes, but I promise that you're not alone.

We're all in this together.

What a long, rough day we've all had.

How about you pick out a movie, and I'll order some pizza?

...Pizza?

Thanks to your help, I was able to send my grandson that last album in time for his birthday.

Did he like it?

I haven't heard from him yet.

Oh.

You worked so hard on it. I hope he knows that.

I think his mind is full of more important things, now that he's in college.

It's the sort of gift that he'll appreciate more as he gets older.

And, after all, I also do this for myself.

These albums help me remember, but it's more than that. I can keep things the way I hope my family will remember them, too.

I'm curating our memories through these time capsules.

Is...is Nicholas's bedroom a time capsule, too? To lock away the bad memories?

Yes, that sounds about right. At least, that's how it was at first.

But now that Nicky's grown up with his own family, it's not as hard to think back on that time.

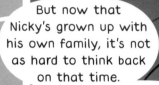

Sometimes I wonder if it was the best choice, but I think it helped us move on with our lives. To heal.

I think I get it.

But...why didn't you ever change it? Or get rid of that... that big metal thing?

I'm afraid this answer might disappoint you, but after so many years, I think we all just stopped thinking about it.

We occasionally discuss the future of this house, cleaning it out and remodeling, but for now, I'm content to leave it as is. My children will come home when they're ready, and we'll deal with it together.

Enough about that. I have something for you.

I'm glad you seem to have appreciated *Peter and Wendy* like Nicky did.

It...definitely got me thinking, at least.

A book can surprise you that way.

Ah, here we go.

Speaking of which, there are so many *better* books out there...

Like *these*. I keep thinking of more, but this is a start.

These are *my* favorites.

I don't expect you to read all of these right now. Some you might have to grow into. But I want you to have them.

This is a movie, right?

Yes, it is. After you read it, we can have a movie night and see which holds up better.

These books will challenge you, but it's worth it.

And maybe you'll find something here to inspire stories of your own.

Yeah.

You could even write *movies*. I'd love to see a Harriet Flores picture someday.

Really?

Truly.

Hey, so, Pearl suggested I swing by the library today.

Looks like there's a creative writing group on Thursday afternoons. Would you like to go?

Can I?!

Well, yeah.

This house
doesn't need any
more ghosts.

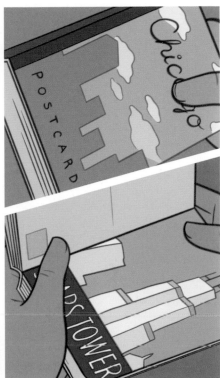

Goodbye,
Ashley.

Are you ready yet, Harry? We have to be at the library in fifteen minutes!

Yeah, yeah!

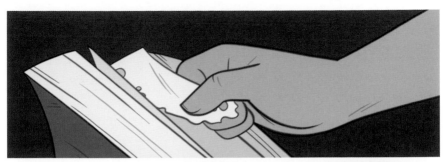

Have you seen the umbrella? Looks like sun-showers.

Got it!

U-um, sorry—

Thanks.

Mm.

Hey.

So, what kind of stuff do *you* write?

Harriet Alejandra's ☆ scrapbook ☆

Me as a baby! I was so cute, what happened?

1983

My parents before they had me! Mom said Papa made merch for her band and that's how they met.

He says they're "straight edge" whatever that is

Fluffy was the best! I miss him.

Summer camp 1995

Halloween 1995

We moved away in July 1996. Good bye, Indiana!

Chicago's okay, it has penguins

Abuelita even visited!

We're ready for the
new school year!

Author's Note

A theme I wove into *Sincerely, Harriet* is living with chronic (ongoing) illness. Throughout the story, I aimed to show a couple of different experiences people might have with it. Harriet has multiple sclerosis, or MS, a disease of the central nervous system. It affects communication between the brain and the rest of the body. In choosing the story's setting, I decided that Harriet's family would have moved to a big city to be close to special doctors that can help her learn how to manage this lifelong condition.

Pearl's son Nicholas had polio, a disease that can cause muscle weakness, paralysis, or even death. The 1950s saw one of the worst polio epidemics (widespread outbreaks) in American history. Black Americans faced strict segregation (the separation of people by race). Many hospitals prioritized space for white children. Families like Nicky's would have faced challenges in getting the medical care they needed.

Nicholas's iron lung, which Harriet sees during her trip upstairs, would have helped him breathe while he recovered. Later, he would have learned how to move again using mobility aids such as a wheelchair, leg braces, and crutches. We don't meet Nicholas as an adult in *Sincerely, Harriet*, but I envisioned that the grown-up Nicholas would have post polio syndrome, or PPS. People with this condition may have muscle weakness, difficulty breathing, and other challenges many years after recovering from polio.

MS and PPS can both be considered *invisible disabilities*, or medical conditions that affect a person's daily life—even though the condition isn't always obvious to other people. For example, Harriet and Nicky use mobility aids sometimes but not always. When someone with an invisible disability doesn't need an aid, other people may forget their different needs. But people like Harriet and Nicholas may still feel their illnesses even if we can't see them.

At the same time, if we asked Nicholas who he is, he'd tell us about his kids, his poodles, and his career as a sports journalist. Just like how Harriet would tell us she loves movies, cooking, and maybe even writing. Their disabilities deserve our consideration and respect, but they don't define who they are as people.

Further Reading

Disability in Kidlit: Honor Roll
http://disabilityinkidlit.com/honor-roll/
This list of books includes many different stories about characters with disabilities.

What Is an Invisible Disability?—The Invisible Disabilities Association
https://invisibledisabilities.org/what-is-an-invisible-disability
This page from the Invisible Disabilities Association shares more about how to define invisible disability.

Author Acknowledgments

Tremendous gratitude to the Associates of the Boston Public Library, for the residency where this seed first began to take root; M, M, J, and C, for sharing your experiences so generously and for holding me accountable; the Graphic Novel Workshop at CCS, for pushing this little story to its fullest potential; my agent, Jen, for teaching and protecting me so well; my editor, Greg, for taking a chance on me, and the whole team at Lerner, for making this book the best it can be; my comics cohort, including Niki, Kori, Lora, Melanie, Ali, and so many more, for the constant flow of inspiration, wisdom, and support; and my precious family and friends all across the world, including my partner, David, whose love and understanding sustain me every single day. Thank you.

About the Author

Sarah Winifred Searle originally hails from spooky New England but currently lives in sunny Perth, Australia. She's known for graphic memoirs and fiction inspired by history and the connections between people. When she isn't writing and drawing comics, Sarah's favorite things are planning Dungeons & Dragons adventures with her partner, rainy days with their foster cats, and naming the lizards and bugs that live in their garden. Find her at swinsea.com.